SECRET AGENT

# JACK STALWART

# The Search for the Sunken Treasure: AUSTRALIA

Join Secret Agent Jack Stalwart

on his other adventures:


The Escape of the Deadly Dinosaur: **USA**

The Mystery of the Mona Lisa: **FRANCE**

The Secret of the Sacred Temple: **CAMBODIA**

# The Search for the Sunken Treasure: AUSTRALIA

Elizabeth Singer Hunt

Illustrated by Brian Williamson

RED FOX

THE SEARCH FOR THE SUNKEN TREASURE: AUSTRALIA
A RED FOX BOOK 978 1 862 30125 2

First published in Great Britain by Red Fox,
an imprint of Random House Children's Publishers UK

This edition published 2006

14

Set in Meta, Trixie, American Typewriter, Luggagetag,
Gill Sans Condensed and Serpentine.

Red Fox Books are published by Random House Children's Publishers UK
61–63 Uxbridge Road, London W5 5SA,
A Random House Group Company

Addresses for companies within The Random House Group Limited
can be found at:
www.randomhouse.co.uk/offices.htm

THE RANDOM HOUSE GROUP Limited Reg. No. 954009
**www.randomhousechildrens**.co.uk

A CIP catalogue record for this book is available from the British Library.

The Random House Group Limited supports The Forest Stewardship
Council® (FSC®), the leading international forest-certification organisation.
Our books carrying the FSC label are printed on FSC®-certified paper.
FSC is the only forest-certification scheme supported by the leading
environmental organisations, including Greenpeace. Our
paper procurement policy can be found at
www.randomhouse.co.uk/environment

Printed and bound in Great Britain by Clays Ltd, St Ives plc

*For Rachel, Josh, Andy, Suzi and*
*all of our Australian friends*

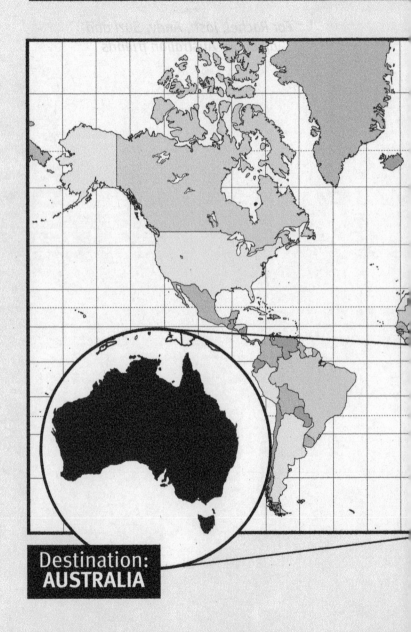

Destination:
**AUSTRALIA**

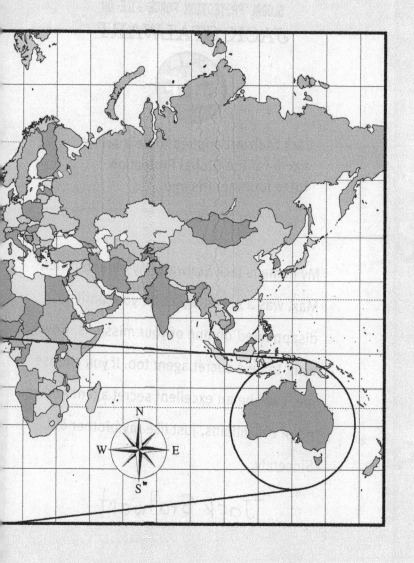

# JACK STALWART

Jack Stalwart applied to be a secret
agent for the Global Protection
Force four months ago.

My name is Jack Stalwart. My older brother,

Max, was a secret agent for you, until he

disappeared on one of your missions. Now I

want to be a secret agent too. If you choose

me, I will be an excellent secret agent and get

rid of evil villains, just like my brother did.

Sincerely,

Jack Stalwart

GLOBAL PROTECTION FORCE INTERNAL MEMO:

# HIGHLY CONFIDENTIAL

Jack Stalwart was sworn in as a Global Protection Force secret agent four months ago. Since that time, he has completed all of his missions successfully and has stopped no less than twelve evil villains. Because of this he has been assigned the code name 'COURAGE'.

Jack has yet to uncover the whereabouts of his brother, Max, who is still working for this organization at a secret location. Do not give Secret Agent Jack Stalwart this information. He is never to know about his brother.

*Gerald Barter*

Gerald Barter
Director, Global Protection Force

# THINGS YOU'LL FIND IN EVERY BOOK

**Watch Phone:** The only gadget Jack wears all the time, even when he's not on official business. His Watch Phone is the central gadget that makes most others work. There are lots of important features, most importantly the 'C' button, which reveals the code of the day – necessary to unlock Jack's Secret Agent Book Bag. There are buttons on both sides, one of which ejects his life-saving Melting Ink Pen. Beyond these functions, it also works as a phone and, of course, gives Jack the time of day.

**Global Protection Force (GPF):** The GPF is the organization Jack works for. It's a worldwide force of young secret agents whose aim is to protect the world's people, places and possessions. No one knows exactly where its main offices are located (all correspondence and gadgets for repair are sent to a special PO Box, and training is held at various locations around the world), but Jack thinks it's somewhere cold, like the Arctic Circle.

**Whizzy:** Jack's magical miniature globe. Almost every night at precisely 7:30 p.m., the GPF uses Whizzy to send Jack the identity of the country that he must travel to. Whizzy can't talk, but he can cough up messages. Jack's parents don't know Whizzy is anything more than a normal globe.

**The Magic Map:** The magical map hanging on Jack's bedroom wall. Unlike most maps, the GPF's map is made of a mysterious wood. Once Jack inserts the country piece from Whizzy, the map swallows Jack whole and sends him away on his missions. When he returns, he arrives precisely one minute after he left.

**Secret Agent Book Bag:** The Book Bag that Jack wears on every adventure. Licensed only to GPF secret agents, it contains top-secret gadgets necessary to foil bad guys and escape certain death. To activate the bag before each mission, Jack must punch in a secret code given to him by his Watch Phone. Once he's away, all he has to do is place his finger on the zip, which identifies him as the owner of the bag and immediately opens.

# THE STALWART FAMILY

### Jack's dad, John

He moved the family to England
when Jack was two, in order to take
a job with an aerospace company.
As far as Jack knows, his dad designs and
manufactures aeroplane parts. Jack's dad thinks
he is an ordinary boy and that his other son, Max,
attends a school in Switzerland. Jack's dad is
American and his mum is British, which makes
Jack a bit of both.

### Jack's mum, Corinne

One of the greatest mums as far as
Jack is concerned. When she and her
husband received a letter from a
posh school in Switzerland inviting Max to attend,
they were overjoyed. Since Max left six months ago,
they have received numerous notes in Max's
handwriting telling them he's OK. Little do they know
it's all a lie and that it's the GPF sending those letters.

### Jack's older brother, Max

Two years ago, at the age of nine, Max joined the GPF. Max used to tell Jack about his adventures and show him how to work his secret-agent gadgets. When the family received a letter inviting Max to attend a school in Europe, Jack figured it was to do with the GPF. Max told him he was right, but that he couldn't tell Jack anything about why he was going away.

### Nine-year-old Jack Stalwart

Four months ago, Jack received an anonymous note saying: 'Your brother is in danger. Only you can save him.' As soon as he could, Jack applied to be a secret agent too. Since that time, he's battled some of the world's most dangerous villains, and hopes some day in his travels to find and rescue his brother, Max.

# DESTINATION:
## *Australia*

Mainland Australia was first settled by Aboriginal people about 50,000 years ago. Many came from Southeast Asia

•

On 26 January 1788, ships from Great Britain landed in present-day Sydney. They were carrying migrants and convicts. The date of this landing is celebrated in Australia as Australia's National Day

•

Australia is a diverse continent made up of deserts, tropical rainforests, snow-capped mountains and forests

Over twenty million people live on the continent of Australia today

•

Canberra is the capital city

•

Australia is divided into six states (New South Wales, Queensland, South Australia, Tasmania, Victoria, Western Australia) and two territories (Northern Territory and Australian Capital Territory)

•

Although Australia has a prime minister, its head of state is the Queen of England (Queen Elizabeth II)

# THINGS EVERY SECRET AGENT SHOULD KNOW ABOUT HMS PANDORA

HMS Pandora was a British warship

•

It set sail on 7 November 1790 from Portsmouth, England, in search of men who had 'hijacked' HMS Bounty. These hijackers were called 'mutineers'

•

After finding the mutineers in Tahiti, HMS Pandora headed back to England

•

The ship sank on 29 August 1791, as it hit the Great Barrier Reef during a violent storm. Thirty-five people died, including four of the prisoners

•

The wreck lies sixty-five nautical miles off the northern coast of Australia and is thirty metres below the surface

•

The front of the boat is called the bow (sounds like cow). The back of the boat is called the stern

# SECRET AGENT GADGET INSTRUCTION MANUAL

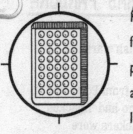

**Anti-Puke Pills:** Whenever you feel as if you're going to be sick, just pop two of these pills into your mouth and swallow (with water, if available). Its active ingredients will calm the sickness and bring you back to normal within minutes.

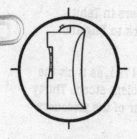

**Dozing Spray:** Perfect when you need to put your enemy to sleep. Just hold the canister up to their nose and push the trigger. A fine mist will spray out, sending them into a deep doze within seconds.

MAXIMUM DOZE: 10–15 minutes

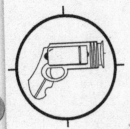

**Spray Gun:** A hand-held gun capable of stopping your opponent or saving your life. Just load one of the five vials found in the Vial Box (see below) and pull the trigger. You can also switch from 'spray' to 'syringe' if you need to inject something.

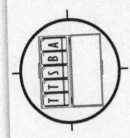

**Vial Box:** A metal box containing the five vials used with the Spray Gun (see above). Each vial is marked with a letter and filled with a different liquid:

A: antibiotic
B: blood
(matched to the secret agent's blood type)
S: steroid (for temporary muscle power)
T: tranquillizer (x2)

# Chapter 1:
# The Reef

Eighteen-year-old Alfie Doyle stood at the back of the boat in his favourite blue wetsuit and looked out over the rough Australian sea. He fastened his oxygen tank, put his mouthpiece in and took a deep breath before jumping off.

*SPLASH!*

He crashed into the churning waves. Almost instantly, he began to sink. He checked his oxygen levels and glanced at his watch. There was only twenty minutes to swim to the bottom, do a bit of research and get back to the boat before he ran out of air.

Ready, he tipped his head forward and plunged into the depths. As he descended, he swam past some of the Great Barrier Reef's amazing sea life. There were orange clown fish, purple and yellow surgeonfish, schools of blue-green puller fish and even brownish moray eels. This was the bit Alfie loved most – swimming with some of the most unusual sea creatures in the world.

Alfie continued downwards. As he approached the seabed, he flicked on his underwater torch. When his feet touched the bottom, he lifted his hand to his mouthpiece and switched on his Underwater Communications Piece.

'Touchdown,' said Alfie into the UCP. 'Will report everything as I go.' In his earpiece he could hear Harry, his boss, who was still on the boat.

'Good,' said Harry. 'Let's hope the sands haven't shifted that much.'

Alfie swam to the back of the wreck, or the stern. Last time they were there, he and Harry had discovered some pieces from the officers' quarters. From what Alfie could tell everything was as they left it forty-eight hours ago.

He carried on, swimming the length of the rotted wooden boat towards the bow at the front. The bow was where the crew members would have lived, and

3

Harry in particular was keen to see what was there. Today their job was to remove the sand covering the bow, bring up any relics and hand them over to the State Maritime Museum.

As Alfie raised his torch to survey the scene, he gasped. The sand that had covered the front of the wreck two days ago was no longer there. He swam a bit closer and noticed a hole going down into the area where the crew members' quarters would have been.

Alfie frantically spoke into his UCP. 'Harry, something's wrong!'

'What do you mean?' asked Harry.

'Something's not right,' said Alfie. 'There's no sand!'

As Alfie was talking, a dark figure in diving gear snuck up behind him. The stranger lifted a gun and pointed their spear directly at him.

'I think someone's taken something from HMS *Pandora*!' said Alfie, his eyes bulging with panic.

Just then, the figure pulled the trigger, releasing the deadly spear into Alfie's leg.

'Owww!' howled Alfie, blinded by the pain.

'Alfie! Alfie!' Harry called into his speaker. But there was no reply, just a crackling noise from Alfie's UCP.

## Chapter 2:
## The Competition

At the same time, but in a different place, nine-year-old Jack Stalwart stood on top of a square swimmer's block in his lucky blue swim trunks and looked out over the indoor pool. He was in lane number three and about to dive into the most important swimming race of his young life – the fifty-metre breaststroke.

Jack was a member of the Surrey Sharks, the county team of swimmers that had won the national swimming competition for the past five years. It was

Jack's first time representing the Sharks in the breaststroke and he was hoping he wouldn't let them down.

He glanced to his left. In lane four was Rusty Sanders, winner of last year's event. Rusty was bigger and more muscular than Jack and was listed as the county favourite to triumph again this year. Rusty was also a miserable bully.

When Jack and Rusty entered the arena, Rusty spat at him, growled and called him a 'loser'. Beyond wanting to win for the county of Surrey, Jack wanted to win in order to wipe the smirk off of Rusty Sanders's face.

The official walked to the edge of the pool and drew his starting pistol. He lifted it high in the air.

'On your marks,' he said loudly. The swimmers bent down to touch their toes.

'Get set,' he yelled. Jack took a deep breath.

'Go!' he hollered as he pulled the trigger on the gun, sending a loud, sharp pop through the air.

Jack threw himself forward and dived, head first, into the pool. A thunderous noise entered his ears as he plunged underwater.

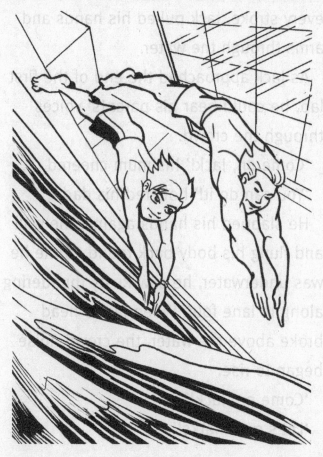

Thrusting with his arms, he pulled his head to the surface. He took his first breath and then looked to the side. Rusty was already a body's length ahead.

'Go! Go!' Jack could hear the crowd screaming. With all his might and with every stroke, Jack pulled his hands and arms through the water.

As Jack approached the end of the first lap, he could hear his parents' voices through the crowd.

'Come on, Jack!' his mum cheered.

'You can do it!' hollered his dad.

He slapped his hands against the wall and flung his body back round. While he was underwater, he saw Rusty thundering along in lane four. When Jack's head broke above the water, the crowd noise began to rise.

'Come on, Jack!'

'Let's go, Sharks!'

Jack was really swimming now. His muscles were burning and his arms ached. He was neck and neck with Rusty,

their heads bobbing up and down, and the finish line was only metres away.

With all the strength he could muster, Jack pulled and pushed his arms. When he reached the wall, he slapped his hands hard. Within a fraction of a second, Rusty did too. But Jack was first. Jack had won! The crowd went wild!

The announcer's voice boomed throughout the arena. 'Our new national champion in the fifty-metre breaststroke with a time of thirty-eight seconds is Jack Stalwart!' The supporters roared with delight.

Jack looked over at Rusty and put out his hand for a polite handshake. But Rusty sneered, leaped out of the pool and made his way towards the locker room. It

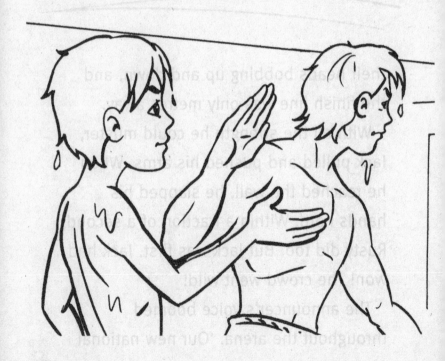

didn't matter to Jack that Rusty was miffed. He'd proven to himself and to Rusty that he was the better swimmer.

Jack looked across the pool at his parents, who were jumping up and down with glee. Then he glanced across to the clock on the wall. It was 7:00 p.m.

Yikes, thought Jack. I'd better get changed.

Jack jumped out of the pool and walked across to the boys' changing room. On the way he was grabbed by reporters who wanted his picture for the local paper, the *Surrey Tribune*. Jack smiled politely and posed for the photos. He quickly showered, changed his clothes and met his mum and dad outside. On the drive home, his parents couldn't stop talking about Jack's triumphant win. But all Jack could think about was the time.

He looked at his Watch Phone. It was

7:20 p.m. Luckily for him, his dad knew plenty of short cuts and by 7:26 p.m. they had pulled into the drive. Pretending he needed a soak in the bath, Jack kissed his parents goodnight and bounded up the stairs. As he opened his bedroom door, the clock in the hall chimed 7:30 p.m.

# Chapter 3:
# The Land of Oz

Closing the door behind him, Jack walked over to his bed. He sat on it for a few seconds thinking how tired he actually was. He hadn't pushed his body that hard in a while and he figured it was going to take some time for it to recover. But, of course, there was never any rest for a GPF secret agent.

Just then, Jack heard a noise from his bedside table. Whizzy, Jack's magical miniature globe, was starting to spin. Whizzy whirled and twirled until he couldn't do it any more and coughed – Ahem! An enormous jigsaw piece in the shape of a country spewed out of his mouth. Jack bent down to the floor and picked it up.

Almost immediately, he recognized its shape. Not only was it the shape of a country, it was also the shape of one of the seven continents. There was only one place in the world that could claim that honour.

Jack walked over to the giant map of the world that hung on his wall. Unlike most world maps which were made of paper, Jack's was a special one made of wood.

Each one of the 150-plus countries was carved and painted in their very own colour. Whenever Jack placed the piece in the right spot, it revealed the location of Jack's next mission and transported him there.

Jack lifted the piece from Whizzy and put it in the lower right-hand corner. Immediately, it slotted in. As expected, the name 'AUSTRALIA' flashed in the middle.

Cool! thought Jack. I've never been to Australia before.

He rushed over to his bed and dropped to his knees. He grabbed underneath for his Secret Agent Book Bag. Hitting the 'C' button on his Watch Phone, he accessed the code of the day – R-E-E-F – and keyed it into the lock on his bag. Instantly, it popped opened, revealing a host of gadgets inside. The Oxygen Exchanger, the Morphing Suit and The Egg were all there. He threw the bag on his back and tugged the straps tight.

From deep inside Australia, a beautiful blue light began to glow. When the time was right, Jack hollered, 'Off to Australia!' and the light burst, swallowing Jack into the Magic Map.

# Chapter 4:
# The Explorer

When Jack arrived, he found himself on the deck of a boat that was bobbing up and down in the middle of the ocean. The boat lurched forward and a spray of water leaped from the sea and slapped Jack in the face.

Funny, Jack thought as he wiped the water from his eyes, this wasn't the Australia I was expecting. I was looking forward to seeing the 'outback', some crocs and a few kangaroos.

*SWOOSH!*

A horrible noise came from the back of the boat. Immediately, Jack ducked and looked in the direction of the sound. As far as he could tell, he was the only one onboard. Slowly, he crept towards the rear and onto a platform hanging from the back. He peered over the edge and into the sea. There was nothing to see but the ocean's dark water. As Jack stared at the waves, he began to feel sick. He reached into his Book Bag and pulled out a packet of Anti-Puke Pills. He popped two into his mouth and swallowed them quickly, so he wouldn't hurl all over the deck.

*SWOOSH!*

There was the noise again. This time a spray of water shot

up in front of the platform. Jack's eyes widened as a round, black object surfaced from underneath the sea.

The object turned round and then looked at Jack. It was, in fact, a diver's head, and now he was climbing onto the boat. Jack readied himself in case of attack, while the diver climbed onto the platform and took off his mask.

'G'day, mate!' he said, with a smile and a wink. 'My name is Harry Pearson,' he added, thrusting his hand out towards Jack's. 'You must be Jack.'

Jack paused and looked at Harry. He was tall and thin with a square-shaped jaw. Seems to be a friendly guy, thought Jack as he put out his hand to join Harry's.

'So,' said Jack, his arm wobbling at the force of Harry's shake, 'what seems to be the problem?'

'Well,' said Harry, sighing as he took off his equipment. 'We could use your help. You see,' he explained, 'the boat that we're on is called the *Explorer*. I'm part of a team of divers researching the shipwreck of HMS *Pandora*. It sank here on the Great Barrier Reef over two hundred years ago. We're in the process of recovering its treasures. I say treasures, mind you, but there's no gold. Just pieces of naval history that the local museum is interested in,' Harry carried on. 'We dived down two days ago and retrieved some interesting bits from the stern. Today we were set to 'descend to the bow, but we've hit a snag.'

'What kind of snag?' asked Jack.

'Well,' answered Harry, 'one of my best divers, Alfie Doyle, went down to survey the condition of the wreck this morning. While he was down there he radioed up that he thought someone had taken something from the wreck.'

'What did they take?' asked Jack.

'That's the problem – I don't know,' said Harry.

'Well, where's Alfie?' said Jack.

'That's problem number two,' said Harry. 'Alfie's gone. Totally vanished. I lost all contact with him at 09:00 hours. Could have been a shark attack, of course, but I've just been down to look for his equipment and there's nothing. It's rare for a shark to eat a diver's oxygen tank, so I'm really not sure what to think.'

'That is pretty odd,' agreed Jack.

'That's why I called the GPF,' said Harry. 'To find Alfie and to figure out what on earth happened down there.'

'I'll get to the bottom of this,' said Jack, trying to reassure Harry. 'The first thing we ought to do is take a look at the wreck. There might be a clue that answers both questions.'

'Great,' said Harry. 'Give me a few minutes to get some more oxygen. Are you a good swimmer?'

'I'm pretty good,' Jack answered. 'I can swim with the Sharks.' He smiled, thinking of his Surrey Sharks swimming team.

'Well, given what's happened this morning,' Harry said, 'let's hope we don't get the pleasure of doing that!' With that, he walked towards the bow, leaving Jack on the platform to stare down at the sea below.

# Chapter 5:
# The Preparation

After a few minutes, Harry returned, carrying a small wetsuit, a mask and a couple of oxygen tanks. 'Here,' he said, passing them to Jack. 'These should fit you.'

'Thanks anyway, Harry,' Jack said. 'But I've brought my own equipment.'

Harry looked at Jack, who was dressed in a pair of trousers and a shirt. 'Well,' he said, furrowing his brow, 'where are you hiding it? In your underwear?'

'In here,' said Jack, pointing to the Book Bag on his back.

Jack slipped off his Book Bag, reached inside and pulled out a small round device that was no bigger than his hand. Coming out of its right side was a long tube that reached round and then went back into another hole on the left.

This was the Oxygen Exchanger – the most exclusive device for underwater agents. It could turn the air that someone breathed out into fresh oxygen, so there was no need to have a tank.

Jack then reached into his Book Bag and pulled out a sheet of flexible black plastic. This was the GPF's Morphing Suit. He wrapped the material around his body and almost

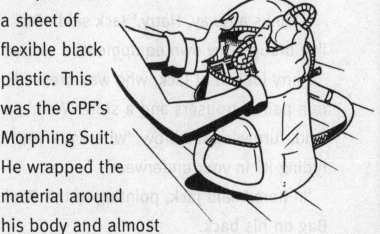

instantly it moulded to form a diver's wetsuit, complete with flippers.

'Wow,' said Harry, clearly impressed.

Lastly, Jack pulled a pair of the GPF's Google Goggles from his bag and put them on. Unlike ordinary swimming goggles, these had a built-in zoom lens which enabled secret agents to see far into the distance when they were underwater.

Jack picked up his Oxygen Exchanger and flung his Book Bag over his shoulders. He tugged on the straps and looked at Harry. 'Well, I'm ready to go,' he said.

Harry, still amazed at Jack's gadgets, stammered, 'You . . . ah . . . ah, forgot something.' He pointed to Jack's back. 'That bag is going to get soaked.'

'Nope,' said Jack with a smile on his face. 'It's waterproof.'

Harry shook his head and slipped his new oxygen tanks onto his back. He put his mask on his face and walked over to the edge of the platform, then turned back to Jack. 'OK, young man,' he said. 'Let's hope those fancy gadgets of yours really work.' He put his breathing apparatus into his mouth, then stepped off the side.

Jack walked over to where Harry had been. He put his Oxygen Exchanger on, took a deep breath and jumped into the stirring sea towards the mystery that lay below.

# Chapter 6:
# The Wreck

Harry was further down than Jack, looking back at him and pointing to a bright yellow rope that hung from the back of the boat and down through the ocean. Jack knew that Harry was trying to tell him to follow the rope so he wouldn't get lost. It was a clever trick that lots of divers used.

As they descended, Jack looked at his Watch Phone. It had switched to 'location' mode, telling him he was fifteen metres under the surface of the sea. Jack continued to follow Harry past the jagged corals of the Great Barrier Reef. He had

read about the reef in books at home, but he couldn't believe how beautiful it was. It was made of all types of shapes, colours and patterns and almost every part of it was lived in by some colourful piece of sea life.

As Jack and Harry approached twenty-five metres, the reef started to disappear, and Jack could see the seabed below. There, covered mostly by sand, was the wreck of HMS *Pandora*. Jack understood why Harry thought it was so special. It was awesome – a mass of timber and iron covered by glittering sand, and lying peacefully on the ocean floor. Harry pointed to the stern to tell Jack where they had already been. Then he pointed to the bow to show where Alfie had gone missing.

Jack swam in to get a closer look. According to Harry, Alfie had said that the sand had been removed and there was a hole into the boat. Sure enough, it looked as if the bow of the *Pandora* had been disturbed. But where was Alfie? There was no sign of him or any of his equipment.

The only way to figure out what had happened was to use the GPF's Time Capture device – a gadget that could play back events that had happened underwater up to two hours before. It did this by tracking the heat left behind from the objects that were there. The Time Capture was even clever enough to tell Jack whether the object was a human, fish or other type of creature. Red meant human; orange meant fish; and blue meant there was a shark on the scene.

When he was ready, Jack waved Harry over. He turned on the Time Capture, pointed it towards the bow and set the time to just before Alfie disappeared, about two hours ago. As Jack and Harry stared at the device, a series of objects appeared on the screen.

At first there were only small orange blobs. Then an enormous red object came into view and began to linger over the bow. Harry nodded to say that this must have been Alfie doing his work. Within minutes another red figure swam up to the first. There was a struggle between the two, then they both swam away.

Jack sighed and looked at Harry. They knew this wasn't a shark attack. When the figures had left the screen they had swum away from the wreck and to the left. Jack put the Time Capture away and then twisted the rim of his Google Goggles to 'maximum' length. His vision through his Google Goggles cut through the sea. Jack could now see up to twenty metres ahead. He scanned the water, looking for any sign of Alfie. But there wasn't a human in sight.

He motioned to Harry that they had to

rise. As quickly as they could, they began to swim to the surface. Jack thought about what he had seen on the Time Capture. Because the colour of Alfie's figure continued to stay red, there was hope that Alfie hadn't been killed on the spot.

But whoever did this was a dangerous person. He or she was obviously trying to keep whatever they took from HMS *Pandora* a secret. Jack needed to be careful. There were predators in the reef other than the creatures that lived down there and no doubt he was going to come face to face with one pretty soon.

# Chapter 7:
# The Klan

As soon as Jack and Harry surfaced, Jack crawled out of the water and onto the platform. He took the Oxygen Exchanger out of his mouth and faced the direction that Alfie and his attacker were headed. He twisted the rims of his Google Goggles again, and his vision shot through the air.

He scanned the top of the water and noticed a small cay – a tiny island of sand – approximately three miles from the *Explorer*. Usually there was nothing on a cay, but on this particular one there was something strange.

Anchored nearby was a large wooden boat. Rising from the decks were three tall masts with climbing nets along the sides and a crow's nest at the top of the middle mast. On deck, several large men were chatting, while others with tattoos on their arms wheeled goods down a plank and onto the beach. Jack knew exactly

what kind of ship it was.

'A pirate ship!' he yelled with a mix of horror and delight. He had only ever seen boats like these in movies and books.

'What do you mean a pirate ship?' asked Harry.

'You heard me,' said Jack. 'A real live pirate ship! Over there, on that cay.' He pointed in the direction of the boat.

Jack zoomed in for a better look. At the front of the ship was a black and white flag. But it didn't have a skull and crossed swords on it – it had a picture of a Komodo dragon, the world's largest lizard.

This can only mean one thing, Jack thought to himself. 'See that flag over there?' he said out loud, handing the Google Goggles to Harry. Harry strapped them on to take a look. 'That's the flag of the Komodo Klan,' said Jack.

'The Komodo Klan?' said Harry,

sounding puzzled. 'Who are they?'

'One of the deadliest groups of pirates around,' said Jack. 'They come from Indonesia, just north of here, and sail the seas between Indonesia, Papua New Guinea and Australia, looking for treasure. They find it and then sell it to make money. The reason they're so dangerous is that they'll stop at nothing – not even murder – to get what they want.'

'And you think they found something valuable in HMS *Pandora*?' Harry asked.

'I do,' said Jack. 'And I think they took Alfie with them.'

'But why would treasure-hunting pirates be interested in HMS *Pandora*?' asked Harry.

'There's nothing down there but bits of naval history like navigation equipment and small personal items belonging to the crew.'

'My bet,' said Jack, 'is that there's more down there than you think. The Komodo Klan is only interested in the three Gs – gold, guns and gems. They don't waste their time with anything else. Which is why,' he continued, 'I have to get onto that boat. If Alfie is still alive it's because they think he might know something. And when they find out he doesn't, they will kill him.'

Harry gulped. 'What can I do?' he asked.

'Stay here,' said Jack. 'You never know – Alfie might find a way to escape and get back to the boat.'

'What are you going to do?' asked Harry. 'It's too dangerous for you to go over there alone.'

'I'm not worried,' said Jack with a confident smile. 'All I need is a clever plan and my little boat.'

'Your boat?' said Harry, looking confused. 'What boat? Don't tell me you have a boat in that bag of yours!'

'Sure do,' said Jack, slipping his Book Bag off his shoulders. 'And it's one of the best around.'

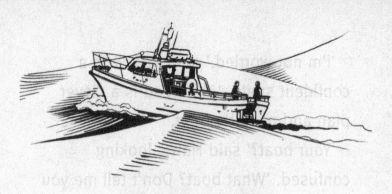

## Chapter 8:
## The Egg

Jack laid his Book Bag on the deck and pulled out what looked like a plastic toy boat. He walked over to the platform and stood at its edge. He dropped the boat into the ocean and watched as it grew into one of the most advanced mini-submarines available to modern spies. Because of its oval shape, the GPF called it The Egg. Its see-through 'shell' at the top lifted to show Jack the driver's seat inside.

'Keep your eyes open for danger, Harry,'

said Jack as he threw his flippers inside and stepped into the floating pod. 'Next time you see me I'll have Alfie and the treasure from HMS *Pandora*.'

'Hope so,' said Harry, waving goodbye to Jack.

Jack pushed the 'close' button on the lid. Knowing that he didn't need to go underwater yet, he set the boat to 'cruise' and the silent engines started up. Staying above the water, The Egg edged forward and headed towards the cay in the distance.

Once he was ready, Jack switched from 'cruise' to 'stealth' and then pushed the 'submerge' button. Within seconds, The Egg started to sink and plunged Jack into the waters below.

# Chapter 9:
# The Approach

As The Egg travelled through the ocean, Jack looked at the dashboard. In the middle was a small screen that told him exactly where he was and where he was headed. There was a flashing green light signifying the location of The Egg and a red one marking the Komodo Klan's boat. Jack tapped the screen twice to target the pirate ship. The Egg adjusted its path and headed straight for it.

When he could see he was close enough, Jack turned off the engines and put his Oxygen Exchanger back on. Then he programmed his Watch Phone, marking The Egg's location in case he needed to find it for an emergency escape. Sliding his hands along the side of his chair, he reached for a small lever and yanked it upwards. Instantly he was ejected feet first into the water through a hatch underneath.

Up ahead, he could see the bottom of the pirate ship's hull and the chain of its anchor. He swam to the chain and grabbed onto it tightly. He pulled himself up along it, climbing one link at a time until he reached the surface of the water. He poked his head out of the water and listened carefully.

'Over here, mate!' said a pirate.

'Where?' asked another one.

'Put it on the sand, by the shack,' the first replied.

'What are we doing with the kid?' said another voice.

'The boss said to hold onto him until nightfall and then we can kill him,' sniggered the first pirate.

Interesting, Jack thought. No one, not even the GPF, knew the identity of the boss of the Komodo Klan. Whoever it was, it was clear that he planned to kill Alfie.

Jack needed to work quickly if he was going to save him.

He switched his Google Goggles from 'tunnel vision' to 'x-ray' and focused in on the boat itself. There were five pirates on the boat's upper deck, stacking boxes and wheeling some of them down a ramp onto the beach. Almost all

the boxes were plain, but on the one that was sitting on the deck, Jack spied the word 'PANDORA'.

Whatever they took from HMS *Pandora* must be inside that box, thought Jack.

Under a hole in the deck, there were several steps leading to a small room. In the middle of the room was a small prison cell clamped shut with a lock. Inside the cell was a person sitting on a chair with his hands tied behind his back. It was Alfie, Jack figured, and he was alive! The Google Goggles could just make out some silver tape over his mouth.

Jack turned his attention from the boat to the cay. There was a small wooden house that looked as if it had been recently built. He could see at least ten people inside. Some were sitting at tables and eating food. A few were watching a small TV while others were working hard to stack the boxes that were coming from the ship. Tilted up against the walls was a collection of rifles and spear guns.

This must be their temporary headquarters, thought Jack. They must be unloading their treasures before moving on.

Between the five on the boat and the ten in the shack, Jack knew he had at least fifteen pirates to deal with. As far as he could tell, none were acting like the Komodo Klan's boss. But there was something else that he noticed – most of the pirates were looking at the shack on the beach. This was the perfect time to make a move.

## Chapter 10:
## The Boss

Jack used all his energy to pull himself up
the anchor chain and over the side of the
boat. Putting his Oxygen Exchanger back
inside his Book Bag, he scurried across
the deck to the hole in the floor, then
lowered himself down the steps inside.
When he got to the bottom, he looked
around. No one and nothing but Alfie was
there. He rushed over to the cell and put
his finger to his mouth.

'Don't make a noise,' he whispered.
'Are you Alfie?' The black-haired boy

nodded. 'My name is Jack,' he explained. 'I'm here to save you.'

But instead of looking relieved, Alfie looked frightened. He was shaking his head violently at Jack. It was as if he was trying to tell him something, but the tape on his mouth was stopping him.

Jack quickly turned round to check the room, but there was no one behind him. He reached into the Book Bag and pulled out his Magic Key Maker. He slotted the thin piece of rubber into the key hole. Instantly, it melted to form the shape of a key, then hardened again in seconds. Jack turned the key to the right and – *snap!* – the lock popped open. He rushed over to Alfie.

With his fingers, he grabbed the edge of the tape covering Alfie's mouth and gently peeled it away. Instead of the thanks he was expecting, a rush of words started to pour out of his mouth.

'Jack!' he whispered in horror. 'There are cameras in this room. You need to be careful! They've probably seen you. They'll kill you if they find you in here!'

Almost as soon as Alfie finished warning Jack, a female voice came from over by the stairs.

'That's right,' the voice said.

Jack swung round. Staring straight at him was one of the most beautiful women he'd ever seen. She was dressed in a black sleeveless wetsuit and had long jet-black hair. Her hands were positioned behind her back. Covering both of her upper arms were detailed tattoos of Komodo dragons linked together by their tails. Standing behind her were two beefy male pirates, with torn shirts and equally detailed tattoos of the giant lizards on their arms.

For a moment, Jack couldn't take his eyes off of her. He couldn't believe 'she' was on this ship with these terrible

pirates. Perhaps she, like Alfie, had been kidnapped and was here with them against her will.

'We *will* kill you,' she added.

That comment shocked Jack out of his daydream.

'You shouldn't have come onto this ship,' she said, her green eyes glaring at Jack. 'Now, you're going to have to pay the price.'

Jack panicked. How foolish he'd been in his rush to save Alfie! He should have known there might be a camera in this room. That's why no one was bothering to guard Alfie – they were probably watching him from that shack on the beach. This woman wasn't an innocent victim after all. She was the Komodo Klan's secret boss, and she was about to kill them both!

Jack watched in horror as she lifted an enormous spear gun from behind her back. At its tip was a dangerous-looking arrow, dripping with green goo. Before Jack could do anything, she lifted it straight at Jack and, without hesitation, pulled the trigger. A deadly spear flew into Jack's leg.

'Argh!' Jack screamed, clutching his leg. Despite the thickness of his wetsuit, the arrow still managed to pierce his skin. Blood began to ooze from his wound.

'That will teach you to come on board our ship and try to steal what is ours,' she said, lowering her gun.

Within moments, the goo released a poison that was soon spreading through Jack's veins. His head felt fuzzy and his body went weak. He dropped to the floor, unable to stand, and then fell onto his forehead as if he was dead.

# Chapter 11:
# The Dragon

When Jack woke up, he was trapped inside a small prison cell on top of the boat. Although the bleeding for the most part had stopped, his leg was still throbbing with pain. He looked at his Watch Phone. It was 1:30 p.m. Just thirty minutes after he'd been downstairs with Alfie. As he panicked, a thought came to him. Alfie! What had they done with him?

Just then a loud clanking noise came from behind. Jack spun round. Opposite him was another cage and inside was a real Komodo dragon. Here he was, staring at the world's largest predatory lizard.

He knew two things about Komodo dragons. One, they were meat-eaters and not picky ones at that. They could bring down deer, wild boars and even humans. Two, they killed their prey in two easy steps. They bit into it first, injecting deadly bacteria that paralysed their victims, then they returned later to finish them off.

'Well, I see you're awake,' said a woman's voice from the other side. Jack whipped round. The boss lady was back.

'Glad to see the tranquillizer gun didn't stun you too much,' she said as she flexed her arms. 'I would have hated for you to be helpless. Woody here,' she added, pointing to the dragon, 'likes a challenge when it comes to eating his dinner.'

Jack gulped. He reached for his Book
Bag, but it was no longer there. In an
instant, he panicked.

'If you're looking for your bag,' she said,
smiling smugly, 'it's over there. We tried
to open it, but the lock is a bit stubborn.
Don't worry, in time we will crack it open
and everything inside will become a part
of our collection.'

Jack couldn't believe this was
happening. Not only had he failed in his

attempt to rescue Alfie, but the GPF's
Secret Agent Book Bag was now in the
hands of pirates! How was he going to get
himself out of this situation?

'I'll check on you in a little while,' the
woman said, turning away from Jack.

'What about Alfie?' said Jack, calling
over to her. 'Where is he?'

'Now don't worry about that,' she said,
looking back at Jack. 'He's in a safe
place. We have plans
for him too.'

Jack watched as she signalled to a
male pirate, and the two of them
walked down the ramp and off the boat.
Jack looked over at Woody, whose two-
pronged tongue was slithering in and out

of his mouth. He grabbed the iron bars and shook them hard, hoping by some miracle they would rattle free. But they stood unshakeable, trapping him inside. Jack thought about Max and wondered whether he'd ever been without a way out. He closed his eyes and thought of Max and quietly asked his brother to send him an answer.

# Chapter 12:
# The Break

Just then, he remembered Max telling him about a mission he'd been on where his opponent had trapped him inside a steel storage locker. The only thing Max had was his Watch Phone. Using the Melting Ink Pen hidden inside, he was able to draw a circle on the door and wait while the inky chemical ate a hole through it. Then Max was able to climb out and catch the bad guy. Jack wondered if his Melting Ink Pen would work on the thick iron bars of the cage.

He lifted his Watch Phone towards his face and pushed the button on its right side. Instantly, a slim piece of aluminium ejected itself. He pulled it out and stretched it lengthwise. He twisted its top until the ink was at its tip and then rubbed it onto the bottom of one of the bars. Jack watched excitedly as the chemical popped and sizzled and within moments had cut through the iron. He did the same at the top, so that when he was finished he could pull the bar down and out of the way.

Thanks, Max, he said silently to his brother as he squeezed his body through

the open space and ran for his Book Bag.
He flung it over his shoulders and pulled
his straps on tight.

'I'm not losing you again,' said Jack,
happy to have his protection back.

He dropped to his knees and peered
out over the edge of the boat and across
to the cay. The pirates were working hard
and the boss lady was barking
commands.

But where was Alfie? He put his Google
Goggles back on and set it to x-ray mode,
then focused on the shack on the beach.
Sure enough, Alfie was inside. This time
he was guarded by a pirate with a rifle in
his hands.

Jack needed to get to Alfie as soon as
possible. But there was no way he could
run onto the cay without being noticed.
There were no bushes, no trees and
nowhere to hide. The only way he could

rescue Alfie was to do it undercover and that meant he needed to vanish.

Slowly, he pulled the Disappearing Milk out of his bag and uncorked the bottle. He sighed, knowing that this would be the only time he'd ever get to use it. The GPF's Disappearing Milk was in short supply and every secret agent only received one dose in their lifetime. Knowing its effects would last only ten minutes and there wasn't another choice, he carefully poured half its contents over his head.

As it ran over his shoulders and down the length of his body, it began to make Jack's body disappear.

He looked at himself and when he was
satisfied he couldn't see a thing, he
dashed off the boat and down onto the
beach.

## Chapter 13:
## The Bold Escape

Up ahead, two pirates were wheeling boxes across the sand. Jack skirted round them and through the shack's front door. Inside the shack, Alfie was quietly dozing in his chair while the armed guard sat next to him, staring in the opposite direction.

Jack quietly reached into his Book Bag and pulled out his Dozing Spray. He walked over to the pirate and lifted his hand. He sprayed the fine mist into the pirate's nostrils and watched as he smiled, and fell quickly to sleep.

Jack pulled out the rest of the Disappearing Milk from his bag and poured it over Alfie's head. When Alfie's body had vanished, Jack gently shook him until he woke up. Alfie was a bit shocked to open his eyes and find his body missing, but Jack whispered in his ear and told him everything was going to be all right.

The two of them dashed out of the hut. Unfortunately, the pirates' boss was walking through the front door at the same time. As they brushed by her, she stopped and tilted her head to one side. Then she looked across to the chair. When she realized that Alfie was missing, she sent one of the biggest human alarm calls Jack had ever heard.

'Komodos!' she yelled. 'Someone has taken our prisoner!' She turned and looked out at the footprints the two boys were leaving in the sand. 'And they're headed towards the ship!' she added. 'Get them!'

Jack and Alfie were sprinting as fast as they could. As they were moving, Jack looked over his shoulder. Behind them were ten angry pirates with knives in their mouths and guns in their hands. As Jack was watching, one of them lifted his rifle and pulled the trigger.

'Watch out!' screamed Jack as he pulled Alfie down and out of the way. A high-powered bullet shot through the air towards the two boys. They collapsed in the sand just as the bullet sailed over their heads.

'Get up!' Jack yanked Alfie to his feet. 'Zigzag!' he yelled, running from side to side. Jack wanted to confuse the pirates by having their footprints dance around in the sand.

Jack and Alfie rushed towards the pirate's ship and up the ramp. As soon they were on board, Jack grabbed the wheel that controlled the rope for the ramp, and started turning it. With Alfie's help, the rope soon lifted the platform off the beach before any of the pirates could jump on. Instead they splashed into the water and fell face first into the sea.

When the rope was secure, Jack turned

to Alfie. Both of their bodies were starting to appear again. 'Do you know how to sail this thing?' Jack asked.

'I think so,' said Alfie, nodding and dashing towards the giant steering wheel in the middle of the boat.

As Alfie surveyed the wheel, Jack ran to the side of the boat. He looked down at shallow water around the cay. Some of the pirates and the boss lady were standing there, shaking their knuckled fists and yelling harsh words. Others were trudging through the water, trying to clamber up the slippery sides of the boat before falling back down. The pirate with the gun was still shooting bullets at them, but there was no way they could hit Jack and Alfie from where they were standing.

'Jack!' Alfie called. 'I'm going to start her up! Can you lift the anchor so that we can get moving?'

'Yes, Captain!' said Jack.

He ran over to another wheel that held the anchor chain in place. With all his might, he pushed and then pulled on the handle, causing the wheel to turn. The anchor came away from the seabed. As Alfie started the engines, the boat began to move away from the cay. When they were far enough away from the pirates and their weapons, Jack returned to Alfie.

'How are we doing?' he asked, placing a hand on Alfie's shoulder.

'Great,' said Alfie. 'I have us headed for the *Explorer*. We should be there in no time.'

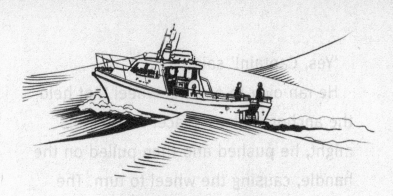

# Chapter 14:
# The Noise

Ah, freedom, thought Jack. He breathed a sigh of relief. They had escaped the clutches of the pirates and were on their way to safety. Jack looked towards the back of the boat and spied the box with the name PANDORA written on it. He had successfully rescued Alfie, captured the pirate ship and saved the stolen treasure. The pirates were trapped on the island with nowhere to go. Jack figured he and Alfie had a few minutes to relax.

'Do you want something to drink?' he

asked Alfie.

'Sure would,' said Alfie, equally relieved to be off the cay.

Jack walked over to the hole in the deck and lowered himself down. He opened one of the cupboards and found a hidden fridge behind the door. Inside were two extremely cold-looking bottles of water. He grabbed them and closed the door with his foot.

Just then, Jack heard a strange noise. *THUD!* It was coming from upstairs. It sounded as if something had landed on the deck above his head.

*THUD!* There it was again.

'Alfie?' Jack yelled upstairs, waiting for a response. But none came.

Jack put down the bottles. Slowly he climbed the stairs and poked his head out of the hole. He looked at the wheel where Alfie had been standing, but there was no one there. The boat seemed to be sailing itself.

'Alfie?' Jack said again, this time a bit more quietly. 'Are you all right?'

'Don't move,' said a female voice from behind Jack's head. His heart started beating loudly as he turned round and found himself staring, once again, down the shaft of a long, familiar spear.

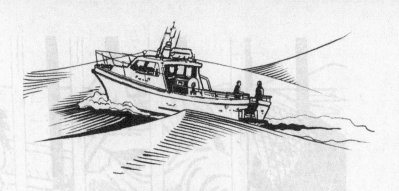

# Chapter 15:
# The Push

'You're clever, but not as clever as I am. Now get up!' the boss lady hissed. Another pirate was standing behind her with an evil grin on his face.

Jack was confused. He'd watched the pirates disappear as he and Alfie sailed away.

'In case you were wondering how we managed to board,' she said, almost reading Jack's mind, 'let's just say, you're not the only one with gadgets.' She yanked Jack up to the main deck.

As he fell onto the deck, Jack noticed
two Human Helicopters lying on their
sides. Max had told him about these
criminal gadgets, which enabled crooks to
fly short distances. That must have been
how they arrived on the boat.

Just then, Jack heard a clanking sound
from Woody, the Komodo dragon. The
other pirate was holding Alfie in front of
its cage.

'Now,' she said to Jack, keeping the spear
pointed at his face. 'I told you before you
should not have come on this ship. This

is our business, and I don't appreciate a
little runt like you coming along and
messing things up. This is the last time
you and your friend come between me
and my treasure.'

'Jake!' she yelled over to the pirate
holding Alfie. 'Introduce him to Woody.
And as for this one' – she leaned close to
Jack and looked at him with her emerald-
coloured eyes – 'I will have the pleasure
of escorting him off the ship and to his
death.'

Before Jack could react, the pirate

guarding Alfie opened the Komodo's cage and swiftly tossed Alfie inside. The dragon let its forked tongue slither out before it leaped forwards to bite Alfie's right arm. Alfie screamed in agony, and then fainted on the spot. 'Alfie!' screamed Jack, trying to rouse him. But there was nothing Jack could do. The Komodo had inflicted its deadly bacteria. Now it would leave Alfie alone while it took effect. Jack, meanwhile, had problems of his own.

'Well,' said the boss lady, 'that should

be the end of him.' She glared at Jack. 'Now, why don't we introduce you to the dangers of swimming in the waters of the reef?'

Continuing to point her spear gun, she motioned for Jack to walk to the other side of the boat where a plank was being lowered over the ocean.

'If my timing is right,' she said, 'the jellies will have been swept into these waters. I'm sure they would love to meet you.'

Jack knew that jellyfish, not sharks, were among the most deadly predators living in the Great Barrier Reef. The Irukandji jellyfish, in particular, was so deadly that a sting from one of them could kill you in as little as five minutes.

As Jack was shoved onto the plank and towards its end, he looked down at the ocean. It seemed as if hundreds of

Irukandji jellyfish were directly under the plank, each one with four deadly tentacles hanging from its bell-shaped body.

Jack closed his eyes. He had to figure out a way to escape from this situation. While he was desperately formulating his plan, the force of the boss lady's foot hit him in the back. He yelled out as she sent him toppling over the end of the plank and towards the ferocious waters that lay below.

# Chapter 16:
# The Jellies

Before he'd been pushed over the edge, several thoughts had run through Jack's mind. The first was that Irukandji jellyfish were known to exist only at the surface of the water. The second was that his Oxygen Exchanger was inside his Book Bag. This meant that, even though Jack held the record for holding his breath underwater at the Surrey Sharks' training pool, he probably only had twenty seconds to recover from the fall, open his bag and get it out. The last was that three parts of his body were exposed to the sting of the Irukandji jellyfish – his hands, his face and his feet.

After he was pushed, Jack tried to remember what he'd been taught about diving off a board. As soon as he was in the air, he took a deep breath and positioned himself so that his arms were covering his face and his hands were pointed as narrowly as possible when he hit the water face first.

*SPLASH!*

Jack entered the sea with a thunderous roar. The momentum from the fall sent him pummelling through the water like a torpedo. Keeping his eyes closed, he counted to himself, guessing how many metres he had dived. One . . . two . . . three . . .

When he reached five metres, he slowed his body down. He opened his

eyes and then closed them again in relief.
At that depth, he figured the jellyfish
would be gone. He was right. He was
surrounded on all sides by nothing but
clear, blue water. And because he
had dived with such speed, the
jellyfish hadn't had time to
sting. But the cut on his leg
was stinging instead, as
the salty seawater began
to seep through the
arrow hole in his
wetsuit.

  The pressure in
his lungs from
holding his breath
was building up. He
needed to get to his Oxygen Exchanger,
and fast. He reached into his bag and
pulled it out. As quickly as he could, he
placed it in his mouth and wrapped the

tubes around his head. He took lots of deep breaths – with fresh oxygen in his body he could now figure out what to do.

He strapped his Google Goggles back on and looked at the swarming mass of jellyfish above. There was no way he could swim into that. The only way Jack was going to be able to rise to the surface was to find a break in the jellies.

He twisted the rims on his goggles and looked into the distance. To his right, he noticed some light beaming down through the sea. Figuring it was a hole, Jack started to swim.

But as he was swimming, something barrelled into his back. It tossed him forwards and pushed the breath from his lungs. He sucked on his mouthpiece to regain his breath and shook his head. Surely the boss lady wasn't down here kicking him again!

*THUD!*

This time it hit him from the side, sending him sideways in the water. As Jack tried to figure out what had actually hit him, a dark grey figure swam before his eyes. Almost immediately Jack recognized its shape. It was one of the most common predators of the Great Barrier Reef – the grey reef shark. And, unfortunately for Jack, there wasn't just one. There were two.

## Chapter 17:
## The Sharks

Sensing they were about to attack, Jack
slowly reached into his Book Bag and
pulled out the Spray Gun. Keeping an eye
on the sharks, he flicked open his Vial
Box and took out the tube marked 'B' for
'blood'. He inserted it into the barrel of
the Spray Gun and then pulled the trigger
as hard as he could. The tube with the
blood shot through the water and
exploded in the distance, far away from
Jack.

Almost as soon as it burst, the sharks

started to swim away. Jack knew the scent of blood would attract them towards it. For now at least, he had some time. He turned in the direction of the hole and started swimming again.

When he finally reached the hole he put his head above the water. He lifted his hands to his goggles and twisted the rims. Already, the Komodo Klan's pirate ship was at least a mile away. He lifted his hand and pushed a button on his Watch Phone. Within minutes, The Egg appeared, just below his feet.

It drifted up to Jack and opened its hatch. Jack swam inside and closed the hatch, then activated the 'pump'. Immediately, the water that had been inside was forced out through a hole, and soon Jack was able to take off his Oxygen Exchanger.

He turned his attention to the dashboard

and punched in the coordinates of his
destination. As The Egg began to move,
Jack thought about the situation ahead.
The boss lady had got the better of him,
not once, but twice. He *had* to capture her,
save Alfie and rescue the treasure this time
around or he'd feel like a failure. As The
Egg cruised through the waters of the reef,
he planned his final strike.

## Chapter 18:
## The Last Try

When The Egg drifted alongside the pirate's ship, Jack instructed it to surface and pop its hatch. But this time there was no anchor chain on the side of the boat for him to climb, so he punched the 'lift' feature on his chair. Slowly, it lifted itself upwards so that Jack was positioned near the top of the boat. Carefully, he looked across the deck.

As far as he could tell, both the boss lady and her pirate assistant, Jake, were nowhere in sight. Jack twisted his Google

Goggles to 'x-ray' and found them below, sitting at a table and looking at a map. They hadn't wasted any time planning their escape.

He looked over at Alfie, who was completely dazed. Jack climbed over the rail and onto the deck, then raced across it towards Woody's cage. He yanked open the door, grabbing Alfie, and pulled him to safety just as the Komodo dragon leaped and tried to bite them both.

But Alfie wasn't moving. Jack put his ear to Alfie's mouth and listened for breathing. It was light, but there was a faint hint of a breath. He was still alive!

Quickly, Jack opened his Vial Box and pulled out the tube marked 'A'. He loaded the antibiotic, switched the gun's setting to 'syringe' and injected the medicine into Alfie's arm. He then pulled out some

gauze and wrapped it around Alfie's arm.

'That should help,' Jack whispered in his ear.

Just then, Jack heard a commotion under his feet. It was the boss lady and she was climbing the stairs. This was the moment Jack had been waiting for. He left Alfie lying on the deck and ran for the bottom rung of a climbing net that stretched to the top of the middle mast. He climbed the net, one rung at a time, until he reached the top.

'Finally,' he said to himself, 'a chance to teach this dragon lady a lesson.' He loaded the Spray Gun with a new tube marked 'T', returned the setting to 'spray', and waited.

# Chapter 19:
## The Stand-Off

Almost as soon as the boss lady emerged, she noticed that Alfie had been moved from his cage. She pulled her spear gun from behind her back and began to creep around.

'Seems we have a visitor,' she said out loud to Jake. 'I wonder if that boy has foolishly come back.'

'Sure have!' Jack shouted from his position on the mast.

In response, the boss lady whipped round and looked up at Jack. Because

Jack had cleverly positioned himself in line with the sun, it was difficult for her to see. She strained her eyes to focus, raised her spear gun and pulled the trigger. A spear shot through the air towards Jack, but he simply ducked and it flew over his head.

She growled to herself. 'I've got plenty more where that came from!' she yelled, pulling another spear from behind her back. She placed it at the tip of the gun and smiled viciously.

'I've got something for you too!' replied Jack, as he pulled *his* weapon from behind *his* back. He lifted the Spray Gun and pointed it directly at her.

'You wouldn't dare!' she grizzled.

'Oh, yes, I would,' said Jack, beaming as he pulled the trigger. The boss lady dived to the right, trying to avoid the vial. But it caught her on her tattooed arm and burst all over her.

'Nooooo!' she screamed as her speech began to slur. Desperate, she tried to lift her gun, but it was too heavy. She collapsed on the deck, dropping her weapon. Then she fell fast asleep as the 'tranquillizing' liquid took effect.

'You little brat!' yelled Jake, seeing his boss sprawled on the floor. He ran for a rifle that was lying on a box near the side of the boat, but Jack sent a tranquillizing vial his way too. It exploded all over his chest and within moments he too was knocked out.

Jack was ecstatic. He scurried down the net and onto the deck. He reached into his Book Bag and pulled out two pairs of handcuffs, then he cuffed the two evil villains to a metal rail.

'That should keep you until the authorities arrive,' he said.

Now that the danger was over, Jack ran across to Alfie. The powerful antibiotic that Jack had injected seemed to be working. Alfie was finally starting to wake up.

# Chapter 20:
# The Treasure

Jack lifted his Watch Phone and called the Australian Water Police. He told them what had happened and asked them to come and take the pirates away. He then called Harry, who had been patiently waiting on the *Explorer* for any news.

'Hi, Harry,' said Jack when he got through.

'Well, I'll be!' said Harry. 'I hope this is good news.'

'Sure is,' said Jack. 'Want to come onboard?'

'Would love to,' said Harry. Jack could tell he was pleased. 'I've never been on a real pirate ship before.'

Within the hour, both the Water Police and Harry arrived. As the authorities were dragging the boss lady and her henchman away, their doctor was tending to Alfie's

wounds. Another squad of police were heading off for the pirates on the cay. No doubt they'd be spending a lifetime in jail. Jack knew the fines for stealing shipwreck treasures were steep, especially in Australia.

'Come with me,' said Jack, leading Harry to the back of the boat. He showed him the box with the word 'PANDORA'.

'Well, well,' said Harry, his eyes opening wide. 'Is this what they took from the wreck below?'

'Yep,' said Jack. 'Shall we open it together?'

The two of them lifted the top of the box and peered inside. There amidst some packing paper was a black rectangular box with gold-painted decorations. It looked as if it had come all the way from Asia. Harry gently reached in and lifted it out. He opened the tiny latch that held it together and gasped.

Piled high inside were what looked like hundreds of gold coins, twinkling and glimmering in the afternoon sun. Nestled among the coins were all sorts of jewels, including sapphires, emeralds and

green-coloured jade. From the look of it, Jack figured the loot was worth millions of dollars.

'Well,' said Jack, happy he was able to give this to Harry, 'I think my time here is just about up.'

'I can't thank you enough,' said Harry, still stunned by the find. 'The museum and I are truly grateful.' He nodded towards Alfie, who was still a bit woozy. 'And I'm sure Alfie would thank you too if he could.'

'No worries,' said Jack. 'It's part of my job.'

He looked at his Watch Phone. It was time to go. He waved to Harry and then made his way across the deck of the ship. He climbed over the edge and into The Egg's chair. Sensing he was in position, the chair began to lower itself down.

Once he was inside the boat, the arched door came over and sealed him inside. He punched a few buttons and a map of the United Kingdom appeared on the dash. After marking his coordinates, he pushed the 'submerge' button. Slowly The Egg lowered itself into the waters of the reef.

From inside the map, a tiny light began to glow. It grew in brilliance until it had filled the entire pod. When he was ready, Jack yelled, 'Off to England!' Then the light flickered and burst, swallowing him whole and transporting him home.

# SECRET AGENT JACK STALWART

## The Escape of the Deadly Dinosaur:
## USA

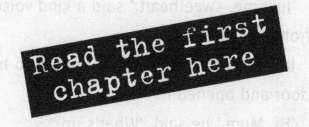

Read the first chapter here

# Chapter 1:
# The Mysterious
# Package

It was almost 7:15 p.m. and nine-year-old Secret Agent Jack Stalwart was sitting at his desk, doing his homework, when there was a knock at his bedroom door.

'Who is it?' asked Jack.

'Just me, sweetheart,' said a kind voice from the other side.

Jack got up from his desk, walked to his door and opened it.

'Hi, Mum,' he said. 'What's up?'

'Just wanted to give you something,' she said, handing him a package wrapped in brown paper. 'It came for you in today's post.'

'Thanks,' said Jack, taking the package. It felt as if there was something hard inside.

'That Book of the Month club sure does send you quite a few books,' said Jack's mum, pointing to the sender's return address. Jack and his mum looked at the address together. It read: *Great Picks for a Fiver*, or GPF.

'Uh, yes,' said Jack nervously, worried his mum might catch on. 'They're great,' he added. 'They always send me just what I need.'

'Well,' he went on, holding the package close to his chest, 'I guess I'd better get on with my homework.'

'OK, dear,' said his mum as she walked away. 'Don't forget to clean your teeth before you go to bed,' she added.

Jack shut the door behind his mum and rushed over to his desk. He sat down and carefully unwrapped the package. Inside there was a book with a picture of a dinosaur on the front. It was entitled: *The Allosaurus: Everything You Ought to Know* by Lewis Porter.

The allosaurus, thought Jack. Why are they sending me a book about a dinosaur? And who is this guy, Lewis Porter? He doesn't work for the GPF.